GAME ON!

THE BIG TWITCH

By Kevin Miller

www.bakkenbooks.com

The Big Twitch by Kevin Miller
Copyright © 2024 Bakken Books

All rights reserved. This book is protected under the copyright laws of the United States of America. This book may not be copied or reprinted for commercial gain or profit. This book is a work of fiction. The Game On series is a work of fiction. Names, characters, businesses, places, events, incidents, and other locales are either the products of the author's imagination or used in a fictitious manner. Any resemblance to actual persons, living or dead, or actual events is purely coincidental.

ISBN: 978-1-963915-07-5
Published by Bakken Books
For Worldwide Distribution
Printed in the USA

www.bakkenbooks.com

Other Bakken Books Stories

Camping books for kids

Mystery books for kids

Hunting books for kids

Fishing books for kids

www.bakkenbooks.com

Math adventures for kids

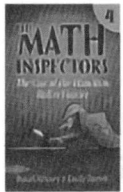

History adventures for kids

Space adventures for kids

Humorous adventures for kids

- 1 -

"Are you sure this isn't too much of a bother, Mrs. Kelsey?" Lucas asked as he struggled to carry a backpack, two bulging green garbage bags, a sleeping bag—which had already come unrolled—and a pillow down the stairs to our basement.

"Not at all, Lucas. We have plenty of room. Isn't that right, Wyatt?"

She turned to the top of the stairs where I was standing with two more bloated garbage bags, one in each hand. I had no idea what was in those bags, but they were *heavy*. Hadn't he ever heard of suitcases?

When I didn't answer right away, my mom's

sweet smile transformed into a frown, followed by a rapid thrust of her chin that indicated she expected me to speak up—now.

"Uh, yeah, loads of room," I said as I started down the stairs, the garbage bags thumping on each step. Not even I found my tone of voice convincing.

"It's only temporary," Lucas called back over his shoulder as he rounded the corner into my gaming room.

Yeah, right, I thought.

"I would have moved in with my dad, but he's got this new job that takes him out of town for three weeks every month, so the social worker wouldn't allow it."

"Like I said, it's not a problem," Mom replied. "You can stay as long as you like."

This time it was me grimacing and shaking my head for her to shut up, but Mom had already rounded the corner as well, unable to see the faces I was making.

I trundled down the rest of the stairs, hoping to catch up to her before she made any more lofty promises, like allowing Lucas to take over my bedroom instead of a corner of my gaming room, but the heavy garbage bags caused me to lose my balance, and I slipped and fell, bouncing down the last few steps on my butt.

"Ow!"

"Are you all right, Wyatt?" Mom asked, her question followed almost immediately by, "Oh my, isn't that lovely!"

I couldn't believe it. I had just fallen down half the stairs, and she didn't even bother to come check on me?

"Do you like it?" Olivia asked, speaking in the baby voice she used whenever she was fishing for compliments.

"Like it? I love it!" Lucas replied.

Wondering what the heck everyone was gushing about, I grimaced as I struggled to my feet, using the garbage bags to push myself up. When I dragged them around the corner, ready to give Mom a piece of my mind, I stopped short. As reluctant as I was to have Lucas bunk in my gaming room for an undetermined length of time while he sorted things out at home, even I was impressed with the transformation that Olivia had been able to pull off.

Scavenging a camping cot from our garage, a nightstand—which she had covered with one of Mom's fancy embroidered tea towels—and an extra bedside lamp, she had created a cozy little sleeping nook for Lucas. It was enhanced by a vase of freshly cut flowers on the nightstand and a colorful *Rumble Royale*-themed poster on the wall that said, "Welcome to your new home, String Bean!"

New home? That didn't sound too temporary to me.

"And check this out," Olivia said, lifting the tea towel to reveal that it wasn't just a nightstand but the mini fridge that was normally out in our garage, full of drinks for when my dad worked out there or hung out with his friends. "Now you don't need me to make snacks for you anymore!"

She opened the fridge, revealing it was packed full of sodas and all sorts of junk food, from granola bars to cheese strings to chocolate-chip cookies.

Lucas stuck out his bottom lip, pretending to pout. "But I love it when you make snacks for me, Olivia."

THE BIG TWITCH

She grinned with pleasure. "Aw, don't worry, String Bean. I still will."

"Um, Oliva," I said. "Aren't you forgetting something?"

She paused to think, then her eyes lit up. I nodded in satisfaction, assuming she had just remembered my rule about no food or drinks anywhere near my gaming setup.

Nope.

"Oh yeah!" she said, bending over to lift the blanket on the cot. "This!"

As if the feast in the mini-fridge wasn't enough, she pulled out a plastic drawer that was packed full of chips, crackers, cheezies, pretzels, and countless other empty carbs.

I dropped the garbage bags on the floor in disbelief. How could this be happening?

In case you're wondering the same thing, let me back up a few steps.

When Lucas told us about his fight with his brother, Darian asked if he felt safe at home. Lucas was reluctant to answer at first, but when we finally got the truth out of him—that his brother had flown into a rage and was only prevented from hitting Lucas when his mother arrived home in the midst of it and restrained him—Darian recommended that Lucas talk to the school counselor. Surprisingly, Lucas actually followed Darian's advice, and things snowballed from there.

Social services got involved, and they recommended that Lucas be removed from his home while his family sorted things out. Unable to move in with his dad and with no other extended family

THE BIG TWITCH

in the area, it looked like Lucas would have to be admitted to a foster home. However, when my parents—and especially Olivia—heard about it, they insisted there was no way that was going to happen. After consulting with me—what else could I say but yes?—they invited Lucas to stay with us until things got sorted out.

As for replacing his computer setup, this time when Shu offered to help him, Lucas accepted her offer. However, he insisted on keeping the monitor with the burnt-out line of pixels down the middle that he had salvaged from the dump. He claimed it was his "lucky" monitor, although how he could think that, seeing as we hadn't even come close to winning a game yet, was beyond me.

So, now Lucas was not only my teammate, he was also my roommate—or at least my housemate. Don't get me wrong; I was glad we were able to help him out, but with Lucas in such close proximity all the time, I wondered how long it would be before *I* was the one who needed counseling to deal with my anger-management issues.

As it turned out, however, the Lucas situation

was only the beginning of an entirely new set of problems that the Stream Team was about to face.

- 2 -

"What do you mean he won't speak?" I asked as the other members of the Stream Team and I sat at a table in the school cafeteria the day after Lucas moved into my house. My question was directed toward Lucas and Shu rather than Darian—who was sitting at our table with a placid look on his face as he ate whatever strange food vegans eat for lunch—because the question was *about* Darian.

"Darian told me—that is, he texted me—last night to say he's just taken a one-week vow of silence."

"A vow of silence? What does that mean?"

"Just what it says. For seven days he can't make a peep."

"What happens if he does?"

Lucas shrugged as he dove into the lavish lunch that Olivia had packed for him. "Nothing as far as I know. It's not like he's being forced to do it or anything. It's something he *chose* to do."

"But why?" I asked, struggling to process what this meant for our quest to forge ourselves into a force to be reckoned with in the world of *Rumble Royale*.

"I don't know. Some sort of spiritual growth thing, I guess."

I turned to Darian for an answer, but he just smiled at me, the peaceful expression on his face putting me in exactly the opposite sort of headspace.

"But if he can't talk, how are we supposed to communicate during the game?" I asked.

"He's not deaf, just dumb," Lucas said. "No offense, Darian," he added. "I mean 'dumb' in the literal rather than the colloquial sense in that he can't speak. But he can still text."

Just then, Shu stood up. "Have to go," she said as she picked up her tray of half-eaten food.

THE BIG TWITCH

"Why the rush?" I asked, glancing at the clock. We still had thirty minutes until classes resumed.

"Big tennis table tournament coming up. Mr. Daviduke want me watch film."

My eyebrows shot up in confusion. "Film?"

"He film top competitor at tournament last weekend. Want me to watch. Find her weakness."

Her English was coming along, but she still tended to speak in short, choppy snippets, something we would have to help her with.

"But we were supposed to use this time to discuss Rumble Royale strategy," I said. "Can't you watch the film later?"

"Have to practice later. From after school until curfew."

"But *we're* supposed to practice after school!" I said, feeling as if the rug was continually being pulled out from under me.

"Sorry!" she said as she hurried off. "Maybe tomorrow!"

My shoulders heaving with a heavy sigh, I turned back to my own tray of untouched food. It was one of my favorite lunches, pepperoni pizza, but my appetite had just disappeared along with Shu.

"Hey, look on the bright side," Lucas said, smiling as he bit into the enormous clubhouse sandwich Olivia had made for him. "At least you and I will have plenty of time to spend together."

Bright side?

It was all I could do not to roll my eyes.

When I got home from school that day and booted up my computer, ready to do a *Rumble Royale* practice sesh with Lucas and Darian, I was surprised to find a friend request waiting for me on Discord. In case you're wondering, it wasn't the fact that I *had* a friend request that surprised me. It was who the friend request was from. Thinking it must be a scam, I googled the username to confirm it was legit.

"Holy cow," I exclaimed a moment later, unable to believe my eyes.

Lucas, who was seated at his own gaming setup on the other side of the room with his back to me, pulled one of his headphones away from his ear. "What's up?"

THE BIG TWITCH

"Oh, nothing," I said, moving my body so it blocked my monitor, for some reason wanting to keep the invitation a secret.

When he turned back to his game, I accepted the friend request, then shot the person a one-word greeting before I booted up the *Rumble Royale* server, not at all expecting a response. The invite was from such a big-time streamer that I figured it was probably part of a social media marketing campaign, and the streamer had only followed me in the hope that I would follow him back, after which he would quietly unfollow me. But to my surprise, seconds after I sent my message, my headphones pinged with a response.

Yo, clutch play in the Royale Rumble Cup the other day.

Glancing over my shoulder to make sure Lucas wasn't watching, I typed a reply.

Thanks! U2 And congrats on the win, btw.
Tks. So, I wondered if I could ask u something.
Sure.
How committed are you to the Stream Team?

"Yo, Wyatt, what's the holdup?" Lucas asked, his voice in my headphones nearly causing me to jump out of my skin.

"Uh, nothing," I said. "That is, I need a few minutes to do something first, okay? Why don't you and Darian hop into a game without me?"

"Suit yourself," Lucas replied. "Yo, Tofu Tater, you hear that? Or were you too busy trying to reach nirvana? Type two X's for yes and one for no."

I couldn't help but smirk. "Can't he just type 'yes' or 'no'? He took a vow of silence, not a vow against typing."

"Hey, you do things your way, and I'll do things mine, all right?" Lucas replied.

"Whatever," I said, not wanting to prolong the conversation.

As soon as Lucas was distracted again, I resumed my chat.

What do u mean?

I mean I have an opening coming up on my Rumble Royale squad . . . and I'd like you to try out for it.

I nearly fell out of my chair. Was this really happening?

So, whaddaya say?

With a quick peek over my shoulder to make absolutely certain Lucas couldn't see what I was typing, I banged out my response. It didn't take long, seeing as it consisted of only three letters.

YES!

- 3 -

The moment I accepted the invitation to try out for the professional streamer's *Rumble Royale* squad, I felt torn. On the one hand, I was super excited. It was every gamer's dream come true—the very reason I had started the Stream Team in the first place. I felt like a basketball player who had just been spotted by an NBA scout while playing a pickup game with some friends in a vacant lot after school, and now I'd been invited to try out for the big leagues.

On the other hand, I felt guilty. Not only had I invested a lot of time and effort into recruiting and training the Stream Team, I had also gotten their hopes up about our chances of winning tournaments and making a boatload of cash. For Lucas at least, that second part was becoming increasingly important, especially with all the chaos going on at home. But apart from those concerns, in the midst of our quest to achieve video game glory, something else had happened, something I hadn't expected.

I was starting to consider these people my friends.

That may not sound like a big deal, but I'd never been the type of person to have a lot of friends. Well, if Olivia were listening in, she'd be quick to say I didn't have *any* friends, and for once I would have to agree with her. Sure, there were some kids at school I chatted with between classes, but it was all surface stuff, and we never hung out together outside of school. So, I was enjoying the sense of camaraderie that was developing between my squad mates and me, and the last thing I wanted was to spoil that. Now that I'd had a taste of friendship, there was no way I wanted to go back to how I'd spent most of my life up until that point.

Alone.

But if these people really were my friends, wouldn't they be happy for me if I told them about this opportunity and encourage me to pursue it? Maybe. But would they mean it? When I put myself in their shoes, I had to admit that, friend or no friend, probably not.

Then again, there was no reason for me to tell them anything yet. After all, so far all I'd received was an invitation to try out. And even if I did make the cut, I would be under no obligation to say yes. Plus, before I tried out for the team I was required to sign an NDA—a non-disclosure agreement—indicating I had to keep quiet about the whole situation. So, even if I wanted to tell my teammates about it, there was no way I could.

Of course, I realized the NDA was just another justification for doing what I wanted to do. Deep down inside, I was determined to go after this opportunity no matter what. But seeing as it wasn't a sure thing, I decided to keep going full-steam ahead with the Stream Team as well. There was no sense in burning my bridges before I had to. Plus, with my tryout coming up soon, the more hours I logged playing *Rumble Royale,* the better.

At least that was what I thought. It turns out my parents had other plans.

That was made clear to me at dinner one night. Unlike most kids at school, who rarely ate meals with their family, my parents insisted we eat supper together every night. At the dinner table. No phones or TV allowed. Instead, they wanted us to have *conversations.*

I know. Weird.

Now that Lucas was staying at our place, my parents insisted that he eat supper with us too. While Lucas could be a lot to take at times, I was thankful for his tendency to hog all the air time. As he and Olivia carried on, that took the focus off me. For the past few nights, I had sensed my parents wanted to talk to me about something serious, but they were hesitant to do so with Lucas around. I'd been lucky to dodge the bullet so far, but when Lucas had to miss supper one night because he was having a supervised visit with his mom, they seized their chance.

"So, Wyatt . . ." my dad began as he cut into his

porkchop. He snuck a glance at my mom, who nodded for him to continue. "We wanted to know if you've made any progress in the J-O-B department."

"What do you mean?" I asked, trying to play dumb.

"J-O-B spells 'job,'" Olivia said. "What's the matter, you fail kindergarten or something?"

"Olivia!" My mom frowned and motioned for her to be quiet and eat her dinner.

I sighed, using my fork to roll my peas around my plate. "Not really. I mean, summer's still a few months off."

"But you don't want to wait until all the good jobs are taken," my mom said, swooping in like my dad had just set me up for a one-two punch. "University kids will be coming home soon, and they'll be looking for work too. You need to beat them to it."

"Yeah, I guess."

"Wyatt, we're not backing down on this," Mom said, her voice as firm as the look on her face. "There's no way you're sitting down in the basement every day playing video games like you did last summer. Isn't that right, Richard?"

THE BIG TWITCH

That was my dad's name. Everyone else called him Rick, but my mom liked to use his full name, especially when things got serious. And she was serious.

"Yes, right," Dad replied, though I could tell his heart wasn't in it. Unlike Mom, who thought video games were a huge waste of time, Dad wasn't dead set against them. He had been a gamer growing up too. He still had his original PlayStation 2, which was how I was first exposed to video games—something my mom still hadn't forgiven him for. But Dad knew better than to cross her, especially when she had her mind made up. Besides, he agreed it was time I "did something with my life," as they put it. I know my dad sympathized with my desire to make it as a pro gamer, but he didn't think it was realistic. He thought video games had their place, but it was all a matter of balance.

There was nothing I wanted more than to tell my parents about my big opportunity to try out for the streamer. However, not only did I fear they would write it off as nothing but a pipe dream, perhaps even forbidding me from trying out at all, the moment I mentioned it, I knew Olivia would go straight to Shu with the news. Then it would be game over for the Stream Team, so to speak. Where was one of those NDAs when I needed one? I would have gotten Olivia to sign one that applied to the rest of her life.

"Are you listening, Wyatt?" Mom asked.

I snapped out of my daze, not realizing my mind had wandered.

"Huh? Yes."

"So?"

I looked up from my plate and realized my mom, my dad, and Olivia were all staring at me. "What?"

"Are you going to start applying for jobs?"

"How can I?" I asked, my mind scrambling for some reason why I couldn't. Then an idea hit me. "I don't have a resume."

"Then your dad will help you make one," Mom replied. "Tonight. Right after dinner."

"Tonight? But I was going to—"

"Right. After. Dinner," she said, pounding out each word to make sure the message was clear.

I puckered my lips as I let out a gust of air. "All right."

THE BIG TWITCH

"Hey, look on the bright side," Olivia said, sensing it was okay to chime in again. "If you get a summer job, you'll finally be able to buy me something nice for my birthday. It's on August twenty-eighth, by the way, just in case you forgot."

I frowned and then, when my parents weren't looking, flicked a pea at her with my fork.

"Mom! Wyatt's shooting food at me!" she wailed, grinning with delight that she had suckered me into retaliating, which meant I was about to get in trouble.

Forget the NDA. Why couldn't Olivia follow Darian's lead and take a vow of silence?

- 4 -

Early the next morning, I was hunched over in front of my computer, the only light in the room coming from my main monitor. It flashed with an array of colors as I battled my way through a game of *Rumble Royale*.

"Hey, whatcha doing?" I heard Lucas say over the sounds of battle in my headphones. In addition to turning on only one of my three monitors, I'd also kept the game volume low, hoping not to wake him. Especially since the only reason I was up so early was to get in some extra reps in preparation for my upcoming tryout, and I didn't want

Lucas or the other members of the Stream Team to suspect anything.

"What does it look like?" I asked as my avatar leaped into the air and nailed another player as he was floating in on his glider. "Yes!"

Lucas leaned over and squinted at the clock on his bedside table. "But it's five thirty in the morning."

"That's right," I replied, leaping across the map in search of more targets. "You don't get better at this game by sleeping."

"Actually," he said, yawning as he sat up and stretched. "That's not true."

Rolling my eyes, I braced myself for another one of his long, complicated scientific explanations. He didn't disappoint.

"According to all the research I've read, sleep is an essential component to healthy cognitive functioning. If you don't get enough sleep, your mental performance becomes impaired. In fact, studies have shown that your cognitive performance declines exponentially, which means each day you don't get enough sleep, your brain function declines even further. It's a compounding effect."

"English please," I replied, my fingers pounding my keyboard as I engaged in a box fight with a total sweat.

"It means if you don't get enough sleep, your reaction time slows down, you lose the ability to pay attention for long periods of time, and your decision-making skills go into the toilet. All of those abilities are crucial to gaming, as I'm sure you know."

"Yeah, well, so's practice," I replied, just managing to nail the other kid before he got me. "While you're sleeping, other people—like me—are training, and the more time you put into developing your skills, the better you get. I'm sure you've heard about that whole ten thousand hours thing that Bill Gates talks about."

I hoped that mentioning Gates, the man behind Microsoft and one of the richest people in the world, would serve as a trump card. It might have worked with other people, but not with Lucas.

"I don't care what some billionaire who made money by creating a monopoly that pushed ne else out of the business has to say about

THE BIG TWITCH

anything," Lucas replied. "But seriously, why are you gaming so early?"

"I told you, because practice is important." The alarm sounded, indicating the zone was about to shift, so I started running toward my next destination.

"If it's so important, why are you doing it on your own? Why not get all of us on the same schedule? We're supposed to be a team, you know."

"I guess I just thought if I set an example, the rest of you would follow it."

Lucas paused, and I could almost hear his face scrunch into a confused frown. "How are Darian and Shu supposed to follow your example if they don't even know you're up right now?"

I shrugged. I had no idea. I was making this up as I went along.

Lucas sighed, then threw on his sweatpants and a T-shirt and flopped into his desk chair.

"What are you doing?" I asked, glancing over my shoulder as he booted up his computer.

"What does it look like?" he replied. "Following your example. Something still seems fishy about it, though, if you ask me."

I didn't reply, too focused on trying to make it to "end game." But his comment sparked a flame of worry inside. With Lucas practically underfoot now that he was living at our house, I would have to be extra careful not to accidentally reveal what I was up to.

At lunch hour that day, Lucas kept yawning as he ate the Reuben sandwich Olivia had made for him, one hand on the table as he rested his head on his fist. I didn't want to divulge it, but I'd been fighting sleep all morning too, my eyes burning as if they were full of sand.

"Why so tired, Lucas?" Shu asked as she sat down with a steaming bowl of ramen. It looked homemade rather than something out of a package, and it smelled delicious.

"It's his fault," Lucas replied, pointing his gangly arm at me without looking up.

Shu turned to me for an answer, as did Darian, who was sitting across the table from us. He was still doing his vow of silence thing, but, unfortunately, that only applied to words, not sounds. I couldn't believe all the smacking and slurping noises he made as he inhaled whatever vegan concoction he had brought for lunch. He was the loudest eater I'd ever heard. And unlike Shu's lunch, his food smelled like death.

I shrugged. "I was up early gaming. So what?"

"So what?" Lucas said. "You were doing it without us."

"Like I said, so?"

"And like I told you this morning, we're a team. If you're getting up early to practice, we all should be getting up early to practice."

"Good idea," Shu said. "Work much better for me than nighttime because of my table tennis schedule."

"Wait a second, I only did it this morning," I protested. "I wasn't planning to—"

Darian held up his index finger to stop me, then typed something on his phone. When he was done, he spun it around to face me, and I read it out loud. "'How about we get up even earlier and do a fifteen-minute meditation session beforehand to help center our minds?'" My eyes widened in alarm as I felt myself sinking into the hole I'd just dug for myself. "Wait a second, guys. Let's not get carried away—"

"Done deal," Lucas said, smacking the table. "It fits right in with that whole 'ten thousand hours' thing that Bill Gates keeps going on about. Isn't that right, Wyatt?" He winked at me.

I scoffed. "Oh, so *now* Bill Gates is your hero?"

Lucas shrugged. "Just because he's wrong about some things doesn't mean he's wrong about everything."

Darian typed another message into his phone and then showed it to us. Something told me all this texting wasn't exactly in keeping with his vow of silence, which was supposed to give him a chance to use the energy he usually applied to communication to reflect and process his thoughts in a calm, constructive way, but what did I know? I was a Medi-Tator by name only. I couldn't have cared less about all that mindfulness stuff.

"*If we're going to get up early, we should also have a curfew,*" his message said.

Oh, great, I thought. Not only had my attempt at a

THE BIG TWITCH

secret morning practice session doomed me to early morning wakeups for the foreseeable future, but now it was going to affect when I went to bed too?

"Good idea," Lucas said. "Just like a real sports team. And as I was telling Wyatt this morning—after he so rudely interrupted my slumber—a good night's sleep is a gamer's secret weapon."

Darian gave him a thumbs-up in agreement.

"So, what do you guys say?" Lucas asked. "To bed by nine and up by five?"

My eyes practically bugged out of my head. "Wait a second—"

"Sound good," Shu replied. "I wake up early anyway to talk to family on phone."

Darian gave Lucas another thumbs-up.

"Then it's decided," Lucas said, not waiting for me to weigh in, as usual. It wasn't as if my vote would have mattered anyway, seeing as the other three were already in favor.

Normally, I would have continued to protest, but as I looked down at my half-eaten lunch, my eyelids were so heavy I could have lain down right there on the sticky cafeteria floor and gone to sleep.

Considering all the extra time I planned to spend practicing in preparation for my tryout, which was only a week away, plus the time my parents expected me to put in looking for a job, maybe a curfew wasn't such a bad idea after all.

- 5 -

"Hi, can I speak to the manager, please?" I asked as I stood at the front counter of the local pet store.

"What for?" the gum-snapping sixteen-year-old clerk behind the counter said. "You buy a defective parakeet or something? We don't do returns, you know." She glanced around and then leaned in close, lowering her voice. "If your parakeet *is* defective, a word of advice: just release it into the wild and let nature take its course. But do it at night so no one sees you. And if anyone asks, you didn't hear it from me." She pulled back and ran her index finger and thumb across her lips, pretending to zip them shut.

I stared at her in astonishment, not believing what I had just heard. Then I shook my head to clear it and refocused on my purpose for being there. "Uh, no, nothing like that. We don't have any pets, actually, never mind parakeets. I was just wondering if you have any job openings."

The girl scoffed. "Job openings? Here? Does it look like we need any extra help?" She gestured to the empty store. My eyes wandered from pet food displays to cat toys to dog beds to aquariums full of tropical fish and then back to her.

"Can I at least leave my resume?" I asked, pulling one out of the manila folder I was carrying.

"I guess so," she replied, reaching for it. "If worse comes to worst, we're always looking for more paper to put at the bottom of the parrot's cage."

"On second thought, forget it," I said, yanking my resume back before she could take it. "Thanks anyway."

"Whatever," she replied. "But remember what I told you." She mimed a pair of wings flapping, pointed at the sky, and then zipped her lips again.

THE BIG TWITCH

"Riiight," I replied, drawing the word out to indicate my disapproval. Then I zipped my lips for good measure and headed for the door before she decided to give me any more "advice."

The pet store was my third stop as I "pounded the pavement," as my dad called it, a.k.a., "looked for a job." My first two stops had been at a video game store—naturally—and a skateboard shop. I was working my way down a list of potential jobs that might be remotely interesting and that wouldn't require a lot of physical labor. However, those two requirements were trumped by a secret third condition—that the chances of employment in those establishments be slim to none. Every kid wanted to work at the skate shop, the video game store, and the pet shop, so applying at those places would make it appear as if I were looking for a job when I knew all along that no positions were available.

The problem was, I was chewing through my list faster than anticipated. And the farther down my list I went, the less desirable the jobs became. Not only that, the more likely it was that I would get hired if I applied. Seeking to delay the inevitable, I dragged my feet and took in the sights of our downtown core. But it was so tiny that it didn't take very long. Noticing a second-hand bookstore across the street that probably wasn't hiring either, I decided to head over there.

While waiting for the light to change, I heard a car horn honk. I ignored it at first, but when it honked again, I looked up and realized it was my parents in our van, waving to me. I ran over to where they were parked by the curb, and my mom rolled down the passenger-side window.

"How's the job hunt going?" my dad asked, leaning over the console toward me.

"No leads yet," I replied as I rested my elbow on the side of the van. "But I was about to drop off a resume at that second-hand bookshop across the street."

"Never mind that," Mom said. "I just found the perfect place for you."

My eyes narrowed, and I stood back from the van, immediately suspicious. "You did? Where?"

"Get in and I'll show you."

"But—"

Before I could complete my protest, the auto-

THE BIG TWITCH

matic side door slid open, revealing Olivia in the middle seat.

"Hello, big brother," she said, waving. I scowled at her and then climbed in, the door sliding shut behind me.

"Is this going to take long?" I asked as we pulled away from the curb, casting a longing gaze back at the bookshop. "Because I really should keep pounding the—"

"No need," Mom said. "Your job hunt is officially over."

"It is?"

"Yup."

"How do *you* know?"

"Because I already talked to the owner, and he thinks you'll be perfect."

"You did? The owner of what?"

"You'll see."

"You're going to love this place, Wyatt," Olivia said.

"How would you know?" I asked, my scowl returning.

"Because it's a place I'd love to work."

That certainly didn't make me feel any better.

My stomach continued to clench with worry as my dad turned down a side street and came to a stop outside of a nondescript one-story building.

"What is this place?" I asked, searching for a sign on the door or the window but seeing none.

"Follow me and I'll show you!" Mom said as she got out. I sat there and waited for the side door to slide open.

Could it move any slower?

Instead of going through the front door, Mom led me around to the back of the building. She pressed a buzzer, and a few seconds later, the door opened, revealing a shortish, stocky, middle-aged man with a mustache. He was wearing a white T-shirt, white pants, and a white apron. At least they had started out white. Now they were covered in all sorts of stains, and his hair was sprinkled with what appeared to be flour.

"Ah, Mrs. Kelsey, so good to see you again," the man said as he wiped his hands on a rag that was as filthy as his apron. "This must be Lucas."

"No, this is Wyatt," Mom said.

THE BIG TWITCH

"Oh, well, hello, Wyatt," the man said, holding his hand out in greeting.

As I shook it, I wondered how he could have possibly gotten those two names confused, but before I was able to ask about it, the man continued.

"So, Wyatt, your mom tells me you love baking."

"Uh, yeah, I guess," I replied. "Eating it, that is."

"Well, you'll love it even more once you learn how to do it yourself."

"I will? That is, how am I going to learn how to bake?"

"In here," the man said, gesturing to the dark, cavernous space behind him. As I looked over his shoulder, in the gloom I saw various other white-clad figures scurrying about as they performed various tasks. Their movements were accompanied by the sounds of pans clanging, fans blowing, and mixers whirring. Only then did I realize the air wafting out the door was saturated with the smell of fresh bread, buns, donuts, and all sorts of other baked goods, not to mention a wall of heat.

"This is a bakery?" I said, realizing I probably sounded like the world's biggest dunce considering all the evidence right there in front of me. "But there's no sign out front."

"That's because it's more of an industrial bakery," Mom explained. "They don't sell their products directly to customers. They distribute them to all the local grocery stores. And this is Mr. Bouchard, the owner."

"Call me Marcel," the man said.

"So, you want me . . . to work here?" The question was directed as much at my mom as Marcel.

"What's the matter, son? You got something against donuts?"

"No, it's just—"

"Because if you work here, you get all the donuts you can eat."

That didn't sound too bad, actually.

"What would I be doing here? As you can see from my resume, I don't have much experience with baking." I handed him a copy. He took one look at it and then handed it back, leaving grease stains on it from his fingers.

"No knowledge required!" Marcel said. "You'll learn on the job."

THE BIG TWITCH

"And the best part is, you won't have to fit it in after school," Mom added.

"Oh, so it's just on weekends?" I said, a trickle of relief flowing back into my body.

"That's right," Marcel replied.

"Saturday mornings," Mom added.

The trickle of relief slowed to a dribble. "What time would I have to start?"

"Five thirty for now," Marcel said. "But you do a good job, and I'll let you start even earlier."

"Earlier?" I croaked.

The dribble of relief came to an abrupt stop.

"Isn't that great?" Mom said. "You start early, which means you'll be done early, so you'll still have the rest of the day to do whatever you want. Though you'll have to go to bed early too."

"I go to bed at eight thirty," Marcel said.

That wasn't helping.

"But the Stream Team just agreed to start holding Rumble Royale practices before school every morning," I said.

"Then you'll have plenty of practice waking up at the crack of dawn, won't you?" Mom replied.

KEVIN MILLER

How had she gotten so good at turning everything I said against me?

"Sorry I'm late!" a familiar voice said, causing all of us to turn around. I couldn't believe my eyes when Lucas rounded the side of the building, huffing from exertion.

"Better late than never," Mom said, smiling.

"So *you* must be Lucas," Marcel said. "My, you're a tall one," he added as Lucas, who had bent over to catch his breath, straightened up to his full height.

Lucas smiled as he shook Marcel's hand. "That's what they tell me."

THE BIG TWITCH

"Wait a second. What's *he* doing here?" I asked, my eyes jumping back and forth between Mom, Lucas, and Marcel.

"Oh, didn't I tell you?" Mom said. "Marcel wants to hire both of you."

I looked at Lucas in disbelief. Not only was he living with me and gaming with me, but now I had to work with him too?

Lucas leaned toward the doorway and took a deep breath and then let it out, savoring the aroma. "If I'm not mistaken, that's the smell of honey crullers, isn't it?"

Marcel laughed. "That's right! See? The kid's a natural." He clapped Lucas on the back. "Come on in, and I'll let you try one."

"Yes!" Lucas said. "They're my favorite."

Honey crullers? Only the worst kind of donut ever. Of course they'd be Lucas's top pick.

Marcel led the way into the bakery's hot, murky interior, Lucas hot on his heels. That kid would do anything in exchange for free food.

"Well, don't just stand there," Mom said through clenched teeth as she nudged my back. "Vamoose!"

KEVIN MILLER

Not really having a choice, I followed Lucas into the sweltering abyss, all the while feeling like my dream of becoming a professional gamer was slipping further and further from my grasp.

- 6 -

With early morning *Rumble Royale* practices on weekdays and a job on Saturday mornings that started long before the sun came up, I was in misery—and neither of them had even started yet. On top of it all, I had stupidly agreed to accompany Shu to one of her film sessions with Mr. Daviduke, which would eat up even more of my rapidly diminishing free time.

When I asked Shu why she wanted me there, seeing as I had already proven that I knew next to nothing about table tennis, she said that with my gaming background, I'd be good at identifying weaknesses in her opponent, who also happened to be from Hong Kong. I was flattered by the compliment, but when I arrived at the classroom where the film session was to take place, any feelings of being specially handpicked for the job disappeared as I found Lucas, Darian, and even Olivia already seated there.

"What are you guys doing here?" I asked as I slid into a hard plastic chair, one of several positioned behind rows of tables.

"The same thing you are," Lucas said. "We're here to analyze film. Darian even brought popcorn. Well, popped *sorghum,* actually. Darian's allergic to corn."

Darian smiled and waved as he offered me a paper bag with red and white stripes on it, as if we were in a real movie theater. I peeked inside and saw what appeared to be tiny pieces of popcorn drenched in what under normal circumstances would have been butter, but knowing Darian, it probably wasn't.

"No thanks," I said, forcing a tight-lipped smile. "I'm good."

"You don't know what you're missing," Olivia said as she plunged her hand into her own bag. Lu-

THE BIG TWITCH

cas was happily munching his as well. Even Shu had gotten in on the action.

At that moment, Mr. Daviduke swept into the room, a laptop computer tucked under his arm and his ever-present whistle dangling from his neck. When he saw all of us sitting there, everyone but me munching on popped sorghum, he stopped short.

"What do you think this is, a Hollywood premiere?" His face was as hard and intimidating as ever. "I'm sorry, but except for Shu, I have to ask you to leave."

He didn't need to tell me twice. I leaped to my feet. "Sorry, Mr. Daviduke, but Shu told us—"

"Have you ever heard the saying 'two heads are better than one,' sir?" Lucas asked.

Mr. Daviduke frowned at him and put his hand on his hip. "Do I look like I was born yesterday? Of course I've heard that saying. In fact, I'm probably the person who invented it."

"Well, then think of what six heads can do," Lucas said.

Mr. Daviduke raised an eyebrow. "Do any of those 'heads' happen to know anything about table tennis?"

"Not at all," Lucas replied with a cheeky smile. Mr. Daviduke's scalp turned red, and he pointed at the door, about to repeat his order for us to leave, probably a lot louder this time, but Lucas beat him to the punch. "But we do know gaming, sir. Offense, defense, how to identify strengths and weaknesses in an opponent, and, most importantly, how to gain a psychological edge over the enemy. Play the player, not the game, am I right? Who better to help you with your analysis?"

Mr. Daviduke continued to glare at Lucas.

THE BIG TWITCH

Then he lowered his arm, his enormous chest heaving as he took a huge breath. "You got any more of that popcorn?"

"It's sorghum, actually," Lucas said.

"Even better," Mr. Daviduke replied, smiling as Darian handed him a bag.

"And it's drenched with vegan ghee and Himalayan sea salt," Lucas added. "All of it one hundred percent organic."

"Yum," Mr. Daviduke said as he dipped into his bag and pulled out a handful, which he shoved into his mouth, a few pieces snagging in his massive mustache. He ignored them as he continued to chew. Getting food caught in his mustache was likely a regular occurrence for Mr. Daviduke. And the last thing he seemed to care about was what other people thought of him, especially the students.

All I could think was, *Popped sorghum? Ghee (whatever that is)? And sea salt all the way from the Himalayas? Since when did everything become so complicated? And why does it seem like everyone got the memo except me?*

As we settled in to watch the film, I regretted

turning down the snack, my stomach gurgling with hunger. Even though popped sorghum didn't sound very good, it certainly smelled delicious. But by then I was too proud to ask Darian for a bag.

I was prepared to be colossally bored by the film, praying the minute hand would speed its way around the silver-framed clock on the wall, but as we got into it, I noticed a few bad habits in her opponent right away. When I pointed them out, even Mr. Daviduke seemed impressed by my insights. My confidence buoyed, I leaned forward in my chair and paid even closer attention to what was on the screen, my stomach pangs all but forgotten.

When we reached the end of the session, I was surprised to discover that over an hour had passed. My stomach was roaring with hunger by then, but eating was the furthest thing from my mind. That's because the film analysis session had given me an idea that I couldn't wait to apply to my own gaming career.

Once we got home, I raced downstairs and booted up my computer.

"Don't go getting into a game," Mom called

THE BIG TWITCH

down after me. "Supper's in ten minutes!"

"Okay!" I shouted back. "I just need to check something."

A moment later, I heard footsteps thumping down the stairs.

"What are you in such a hurry for?" Lucas asked as he flopped onto his bed and pulled out a manga comic book. He was totally into that stuff, though I didn't understand the appeal.

"Like I said, I just need to check something," I replied as I pulled up YouTube on my web browser. I went straight to the account of the streamer who had issued me the invitation to try out for his team and browsed through his *Rumble Royale* videos, most of which featured him and his team in action.

"Why are you looking at that guy's account?" Lucas asked. I jumped at the sound of his voice so close to my ear, not realizing he had gotten up and was watching over my shoulder.

"I thought I could take the same approach to Rumble Royale as we just took to watching Shu's table tennis opponent," I replied. "Analyze strengths and weaknesses of some of the top players, that sort of thing."

"Yeah, I get that, but why watch *his* videos?"

"What's the matter with him?" I asked, spinning my chair sideways to look at Lucas. "His team is one of the best in the country. And they're well on their way to becoming one of the best in the world."

"Yeah, maybe, but the guy's a chump."

I frowned. "Why would you say that?"

"Because he just totally shafted one of his teammates. I'm surprised you haven't heard about it."

I swallowed hard. I was surprised Lucas *had* heard about the person leaving the streamer's team. It was supposed to be confidential. But shafted? That didn't sound good.

"Where did you hear that?" I asked, trying not to sound too interested—or worried.

"On one of the gaming forums I follow."

"Which one?" I asked, turning back toward my computer, my fingers poised over the keyboard.

Lucas shrugged as he grabbed an apple out of a fruit basket that Olivia had placed on his nightstand, then flopped onto his bed. "I don't remember. I browse a lot of them."

THE BIG TWITCH

Just as I was about to type in my query to see if anything came up about it, Mom called us for supper.

As I followed Lucas up the stairs, I felt a sinking feeling in my gut over the possibility that the streamer might not be as nice as he appeared. But by the time I reached the top step, I had talked myself out of it. Who cared what some rando said about the streamer in an online forum? The Internet was full of nasty rumors about all sorts of people, most of which weren't true. For all I knew, the person who posted the story was the player who got cut, and he was bitter about losing his spot.

As I took my seat at the dinner table, my stomach reminded me that I had ignored it for far too long. Instead of feeling discouraged by what Lucas had told me, I felt more committed to making the streamer's team than ever. After all, if Lucas didn't like the guy, that almost guaranteed he was a good person, right?

- 7 -

With our first day of work at the bakery approaching fast, I was more determined than ever to talk the rest of the team out of doing early morning practices. But the more I resisted, the more Lucas insisted that we keep to our proposed schedule. I don't think he liked the idea of getting up early six days a week any more than I did. He just enjoyed seeing me get riled up.

The first day of morning practice was brutal. I had turned the lights out at 9:15 the night before, thinking that would give me a solid eight hours of sleep. But my body wasn't used to going to bed so early, so

KEVIN MILLER

I tossed and turned, listening to music, white noise, and the sound of ocean waves on my phone—anything to turn my mind off for the day. I don't know when I finally fell asleep, but when my alarm went off at 5:15 a.m. the next morning, it felt like my eyes had been closed for about fifteen minutes.

When I stumbled down the stairs to my gaming room, Lucas was already up and at his computer—and eating, of course. Whereas I still stuck to my strict rules about no food or drinks anywhere near my computer, his desk was littered with wrappers, empty soda cans, apple cores, and all sorts of other trash. But that was only because Olivia hadn't come down to do her weekly cleaning yet. The things she did for that guy!

"Good morning!" he said, sounding way more chipper than he should have at that hour. I swore he was doing it just to get under my skin.

I mumbled a greeting in reply as I sank into my chair and booted up my computer, my eyes still only half-open.

"Don't forget, before you log in to Rumble Royale, we have to do our mindfulness sesh with

Darian and Shu."

Oh yeah, right, I thought. I had forgotten about that.

"How are we doing that exactly?" I asked, struggling to remember as I squinted at the brightness of my screen.

"Zoom, baby," Lucas said. "Darian just sent us all a link."

I wasn't planning to turn my webcam on, hoping I could use the fifteen minutes to catnap in my gaming chair, but Darian insisted on it, so he could see our faces. Like Lucas, he was way more enthusiastic than anyone had a right to be so early in the morning.

Thankfully, the meditation exercise he had us do involved us keeping our eyes closed for the most part—which made me wonder why he wanted us to have our webcams on, but whatever. I think I did actually doze off at one point, but the calm, soothing voice from the meditation app that Darian was using eventually brought me back.

"*Okay, great session, guys,*" he typed. "*How do we all feel?*"

Surprisingly, when I opened my eyes, I didn't feel

too bad. Except for my stomach, which chose that moment to signal loud and clear that it was on empty.

"Whoa. I hope that not what I think it was!" Shu said. To make sure we got her point, she stuck her hand under her armpit and cranked her arm up and down, just like we'd taught her.

"Nailed it!" Lucas replied. "Wyatt, how could you?"

"It wasn't me!" I said, my face turning red. "That is, it wasn't . . . that. It was my stomach. I'm starving."

I shook my head as the others laughed, unable to believe I had taken the bait yet again. "Anyway, should we get this party started?" I asked, eager to change the subject.

"You bet," Darian typed.

"Okay, meet you all in the lobby."

Minutes later, we were all queued up for a game. Despite the early hour, I was excited to play. Rumble Royale had just launched a new season called Legends & Lore, which was based on Norse mythology. In addition to introducing a bunch of new skins that allowed players to play as mythological characters like Odin, Thor, Loki, Freyja, and Baldr,

THE BIG TWITCH

the map also included several new locations. These included Asgard, which was the fabled home of the gods, and the underworld, also known as Helheim. Plus, there were all sorts of new power-ups, weapons, and other items to collect. They included the Hammer of Thor, which allowed players to leap across the map and do a "ground pound" each time the hammer powered up, the Lightning Bolts of Odin, and something called the Chains of Helheim, which I was eager to try out.

"Any of you had a chance to check out the new season?" I asked as we boarded the War Wagon.

"I played a quick game early this morning," Lucas said.

"Really?" I replied. "It must have been quick. When did you wake up?"

"Early enough."

Darian texted to say he hadn't had a chance to play on the new map yet, and neither had Shu. Only when everyone had sounded off did I realize there might be at least one perk about playing so early in the morning after all—no Olivia throwing in her two cents.

"For those of you who haven't tried the new season yet, this'll be a good time to get your feet wet," I said. "Even though things look different on the surface, the gameplay is essentially the same. But it'll take some time to figure out where the best loot is, what the most popular drop spots are, and how best to move around the map."

I wasn't just eager for the Stream Team to familiarize themselves with the new map, I was also anxious to get as much experience with it as possible, especially seeing as my tryout was just three days away.

"Okay, people," I said as the War Wagon took off with our avatars on board. "Here we go!"

Discord pinged with a query from Darian.

Where should we jump off?

"Good question," I said. "I can guarantee you that Valhalla will be the most popular, seeing as it's the highest spot on the map."

"Let's hit up Helheim," Lucas said. "I was poking around there earlier this morning. I think you guys will enjoy it."

I wasn't surprised that Lucas would choose the

creepiest spot on the map. It fit perfectly with his fascination with Warhammer and other fantasy games. It probably wasn't a bad idea either, seeing as many other players might avoid it for exactly that reason. That would leave more loot for us and reduce the chances of getting killed as soon as our avatars' feet hit the ground.

"Any other votes?" I asked. Not hearing any objections, I decided to give Lucas's suggestion the green light. "All right, the Underworld it is. Get ready . . . now!"

We all jumped out of the War Wagon, our gliders deploying as we flew in formation.

The moment we were in the air, Darian pinged me with a message.

"'Don't look now, but we've got company,'" I said, reading Darian's text aloud, which probably indicated he had seen a few other players leap out of the War Wagon right after us.

"Don't worry about it," I said. "We should be able to beat them to the ground and either run away or load up on weapons and shoot them out of the air."

"Sound like fun," Shu said. "The shooting out of air part."

"So, where exactly in Helheim do we want to land?" I asked, noting that it was a large, dark-gray area with a glowing green river running through, occupying a big chunk of the map's northwest corner.

"I vote for the Ghost Gate," Lucas said. "It's the entrance to the place."

"Fair enough," I said. "Seeing as you've been there before, I'm going to let you take the lead, Lucas."

"All right," he said. "Three, two, one, jump!"

Our gliders disappeared, and we all plunged headfirst toward the area known as the Ghost Gate. My tiredness all but forgotten, I could only imagine what Lucas had in store for us when we landed.

- 8 -

We touched down in the courtyard of an ancient temple. At the center of the courtyard was an altar with a black statue of a scary-looking woman on it. "That's Hela," Lucas informed us, changing his voice so that he sounded like the narrator of a late-night horror movie, "the vicious guardian of Helheim who keeps the living from entering the haunted world . . . of the dead."

"*Scary,*" was Darian's non-verbal response.

"Why don't you go check out that statue, Shu?" Lucas said. My hackles went up when I heard the grin in his voice.

"Why?" I asked.

Lucas ignored my question as Shu's avatar ran over to the altar.

"Now interact with it, just like you would with a chest," Lucas said.

The moment Shu did, her avatar grabbed the statue and tossed it to the ground, smashing it.

"Why'd you do that?" I asked.

"Just listen," Lucas replied, the grin in his voice growing even louder.

A second later, an unearthly growl echoed throughout the ruins, followed by some white words on the screen: "Eliminate the elves!"

"That not sound good," Shu said.

"Dark elves!" Lucas shouted.

"Shhh!" I said. "You're going to wake up Mom and Dad. Or worse, Olivia."

"Too late," Olivia said, speaking through a yawn.

"Olivia? What are you doing here?" I asked. "And how are you here?"

"I'm spectating on my iPad."

Of course.

"Now what we do?" Shu asked.

"We have to kill the dark elves," Lucas replied, "and whoever else happens to land here."

"Then I suggest we start looting," I said, already racing around and doing just that.

Another screech sounded.

"Too late!" Shu cried as a pack of dark elves materialized out of the gloom behind us. "Run!"

We raced into the temple, which was full of twisting staircases and tight corners, but thankfully, there was lots of loot and chests in there too.

"Get guns and ammo!" I said. "Forget about everything else for now."

My headphones pinged with another message from Darian.

Incoming!

"I see them," I replied as symbols flew across the top of my screen, indicating another squad had landed there. As if the dark elves weren't bad enough.

"Aagghh!" someone cried as another spine-tingling screech rippled through my headphones. The voice sounded a lot like Darian, but I didn't have time to ask because three dark elves were right on my tail.

KEVIN MILLER

THE BIG TWITCH

I fired a couple of shots at them as I raced up the steps, managing to kill one. Then I jumped out the window and landed on a roof. I ran across it and then leaped onto a stone bridge that was broken in several places. I soared across the first gap but missed the second, landing in the murky green water below. By then the dark elves were right on top of me.

Executing a nifty spinning jump move, I killed one of them, which meant only one more was left. When I went to shoot it, though, my gun clicked. I was out of ammo.

"Dang it!"

It leaped at me, its jaws gaping, but I switched to my sledgehammer and managed to dispatch it without suffering too much damage.

"The good news is, these things are pretty easy to kill," I said as my avatar raced around in the knee-deep water, picking up the meat and other items that the dark elves had dropped when they died.

Just then, three bullets flew past me, and a fourth one hit.

"Those guys may not be," Olivia said.

"And don't forget Hela," Lucas added.

"What?" I replied as I ran for cover, desperate to scoop up more ammo and loot before the other squad obliterated me.

"She's the boss around these parts," Lucas said. "You don't think she's going to let you get away with killing her pets, do you? Boom! I just fragged the last dark elf."

Right on cue, another blood-curdling screech echoed through the ruins, and Hela materialized in the center of a circle in the courtyard right near her fallen statue. She was dressed in flowing black robes with a chain of bones hanging from her neck. Extending from head head was a pair of long, curly horns, and her cruel face was twisted into a mask of rage. Above her was a caption that said, "You dare to enter Helheim? PREPARE TO DIE!"

"Um, a little help?" Shu said, the member of our team who just happened to be closest to him.

"I'm coming!" I replied, still dodging bullets from the other squad.

All three of us converged on the courtyard to help Shu take down Hela. Not only did Hela have

THE BIG TWITCH

a boatload of health, but she also had a powerful shotgun and a spinning attack move that made her deadly and almost impossible to hit.

"Spray her!" I said. "We've got to take down her health!"

"Aagh!" someone cried as Hela did her spin move and slammed into our group, inflicting damage on all of us.

"Yo, Darian," Lucas said, "doesn't a vow of silence include muting your mic?"

Even I had to chuckle at that.

Suddenly, someone started spraying Hela from another direction.

"Hey, that other team's helping you!" Olivia said. "How nice."

"They're not helping us," Lucas replied. "They're helping themselves."

"How?" I asked, wishing I had done more research on this new map.

"When you kill Hela, you get a medallion that gives you something called Helheim Haste. It's a power-up that allows you to speed around the map. You also get Hela's Guardian Shotgun, which is like a souped-up version of the regular Guardian Shotgun."

"In other words, if they get their hands on those things first, we're dead," I replied.

"Not exactly," Lucas said.

"What do you mean?"

"Whoever *goes for* those weapons is dead because the other team will kill them."

"So, what should we do?" I asked.

"Forget about Hela," Lucas said, his avatar leaping onto an elevated walkway as Hela tried to take him out with his spin move. "Let's focus those other fools!"

"You heard the man!" I said. "Get 'em!"

Surprising the other team, we redirected our fire from Hela to them, taking two players out right away. The other two boxed up to protect themselves.

"Quick! Let's get Hela before they heal up!" Lucas said. Green crosses were already floating in front of their fort, indicating the remaining members of the other team were popping shields and heals.

My headphones pinged with another message from Darian.

THE BIG TWITCH

Sorry I couldn't be more help.

Only then did I realize our attack on the other team had come at a cost. Darian's avatar was dead.

With no time to worry about that, we focused our fire on Hela, who kept taunting us with captions that said things like "Prepare to die!" But we managed to take her out in the nick of time.

"Lucas, grab the medallion. I'll get the shotgun."

"No, you get the medallion. I'll get the shotgun," Lucas replied.

"Shu, why don't you get the shotgun?" I said.

"Already got both," she replied.

"Nice one, Shu!" Olivia said.

"Then let's laser these losers!" I said, opening up on the other team's fort.

With the help of the Guardian Shotgun, we obliterated it, only to discover the remaining members of the other team were long gone. And no wonder. In the heat of the boss battle, I had totally missed the alarm indicating that the circle was about to pull to a completely different part of the map.

"Let's get out of here," I said.

"Aw, but we just scraped the surface of the Underworld," Lucas said. "I was hoping we could explore the entire place."

"Next time," I said. "Nice work, team."

The rest of us got killed shortly after that boss battle, but considering it was our first time playing so early in the morning, I was pretty satisfied with our progress. However, I also felt anxious, realizing how little I knew about the new map. I would have to spend the next few days becoming an expert on it so I didn't look like a total loser when it was time for my big audition. But before I could do that, I had another early morning appointment to keep—at my new job.

- 9 -

Dragging myself out of bed before the sun rose to play *Rumble Royale* was one thing, but doing it to go work in a hot, sweaty bakery—and with Lucas, no less?

Impossible.

"Come on, Wyatt. You don't want to be late on your first day," Mom said, sticking her head into my bedroom for the second time that Saturday morning—if you could even call it morning yet.

"Yes I do," I replied, my eyes still glued shut. "Then maybe he'll fire me."

"Don't be silly," she said. "You don't want that

sort of black mark on your record. Before you know it, word will get around town and then no one will want to hire you."

"Exactly."

She huffed in exasperation. I felt bad for making Mom angry, but when was she ever going to realize that working at some dumb job was the *last* thing I planned to do with my life?

"Come on, Wyatt, don't be such a baby," Lucas said, joining my mom at the door. I cracked one eye open when I heard a slurping sound and realized he was eating a massive bowl of Froot Loops. My parents rarely let us eat sugary cereals, and when they did, we never got to have that much.

"I sure hope there are some of those left for me," I muttered, closing my eye again as I tried to sit up.

"Sorry, buddy. You snooze, you lose," Lucas replied as he shoveled another dripping spoonful into his mouth. "But I saw plenty of Corn Flakes in the pantry."

Grrrrr . . .

By the time I staggered into the kitchen, my eyes still half shut and my hair a mess, there was no time for breakfast, so Mom handed me a granola bar and a juice box, telling me I could eat on the way.

"This is hardly going to get me through an entire morning of work," I said.

"Don't worry about it," Lucas said, clapping me on the back on his way out the door. "Remember what Marcel said? All the donuts we can eat."

Why did I get the feeling I was going to hate donuts after this?

The drive to the bakery was way too short, seeing as almost no one else was insane enough to be out driving that early in the morning. But it also felt excruciatingly long due to Lucas playing his heavy metal music all the way there. That stuff was terrible in the daytime, never mind before the sun came up. Even worse, he talked over it the entire time, explaining the various nuances of the music to my mom as he drummed his fingers on the dashboard. Between the grinding guitars, growling vocals, Lucas's shouting, and my lack of sleep, by the time we pulled up behind the bakery, I felt a major stress headache coming on. I think even Mom was feeling the strain of the early morning wake-up and the ear-splitting drive, but she tried to put a positive spin on things, as always.

"All right, boys, have fun!" she said, pressing the button to open the side door. I arched an eyebrow at her. Since when did people go to jobs to have fun?

"We will, Mrs. Kelsey," Lucas said as he hopped out. "Thanks for the ride!" Of course, he just had to be a morning person.

I waited in my seat until the side door slid *all* the way open. Mom looked back at me. "Come on, Wyatt. All I'm asking is for you to give it a chance, okay? Remember, attitude is everything. Just go in there, give it your best shot, and who knows? Maybe one day you'll want to become a baker too."

I gave her the kind of look I typically reserved for people who were a few fries short of a Happy Meal. "Seriously? I'm not four years old, in case you forgot."

"You know what I mean," she said, smiling as she gave me a playful shove. "Now get out of here. You don't want Lucas to show you up on your first day, do you?"

THE BIG TWITCH

I pondered that as I watched him greet Marcel at the bakery's back door. For once, I wouldn't have minded that at all.

Inside the bakery, it was already blazing hot. That's because the place was full of huge ovens with rotating racks, not to mention the fact that Marcel and his crew had already been hard at work for the past two hours.

"This is where we do the baking," Marcel said as he gave us a quick tour, "and this is where we do the mixing." He led us to another area with a half dozen industrial-size mixers that were churning away making all sorts of dough. Several workers clad in white were either monitoring the mixers or laboring at various workstations. Some were making bread and buns and loading them into pans, others were making cookies and muffins, and still others were making various types of donuts. A few of the workers glanced up as we passed, but most of them were too busy working—and sweating—to care about a couple of newbies like us.

"So, what'll we be doing?" Lucas asked, rubbing his hands together in anticipation. "Mixing or baking?"

"Neither," Marcel replied.

"Tasting?" Lucas said, the question accompanied by a hopeful raise of his eyebrows.

Marcel chuckled. "Nice try. You'll get plenty of chances to taste things later. For now, I have something special in store for you boys, but before you get started, I'll need you both to wear one of these." He held out two clear plastic packages.

"What are these?" I asked, the first words I'd spoken since I arrived.

"Hair nets," Marcel replied. "Everyone's gotta wear one."

I looked around at the workers and realized everyone was wearing a hair net—everyone except Marcel.

"Except you?" I said, trying not to sound too cheeky.

He smirked and then thumped the hair net into my chest. "When you're the boss, you can make the rules. Until then, put them on, then follow me."

After we put our hairnets on, Lucas and I had a quick argument about who looked like the bigger

THE BIG TWITCH

dork, him or me—him for sure. Then Marcel led us to a big silver machine with a conveyor belt and a fan on it that blew air into a plastic bag.

"This is a bread slicer," Marcel said. "Ever seen one before?" We both shook our heads. "Well, prepare to get acquainted because it's about to become your new best friend. I'll show you how it works, then you two can give it a try."

He demonstrated where to load the loaves onto the conveyor belt, which fed them through a set of reciprocating serrated knives that cut each loaf into twenty perfect slices.

"Once the loaf is sliced, gently grab both ends and slide it into a bag like this, then twist and clip," Marcel said, demonstrating for us as a loaf came through the knives. The moment he slid the loaf into the bag and pulled it away, the blower filled another bag with air, ready for the next loaf. "It's that simple. Once you bag a loaf, put it on this rack here. When the rack is full, add it to the stack, then get a new one from here. Got it?"

We both nodded, taking it all in.

"I've slowed the conveyor down for you boys this

morning so you can get the hang of it. Once you get up to speed, we can crank it up, and you should be able to bag up to twelve hundred loaves per hour."

My mouth fell open. "Twelve hundred loaves? That's like . . ." I tried to do the math in my head, but it was way too early in the morning for long division.

"Twenty loaves per minute," Lucas said, "or three seconds per loaf."

"That's right," Marcel said. "My top team can do eighteen hundred loaves per hour, so that's something to aspire to."

Lucas scoffed, always up for a challenge. "I'm sure we can beat that!"

Marcel grinned at some of his workers who had overheard Lucas's comment and shook their heads. "We'll see about that," he said. "Now, one of you can start as the loader and the other as the bagger, then every thirty minutes you can switch, so you don't get bored. Lucas, why don't you load first? Wyatt, you bag. I'll watch until you get it down and then leave you to it."

I didn't like the fact that Marcel had given me the harder job, especially with him standing right there looking over my shoulder, but it wasn't like I could back out now, so I decided to follow Mom's advice and give it my best shot.

The first loaf didn't go too badly. I scooped it up just like Marcel had shown us, then popped it into the bag. I gave the bag a quick spin and then popped on a clip, taking a moment to admire my handiwork.

"No time to gawk, Wyatt," Marcel said. "Put it on the rack. The next loaf is already coming through."

I looked at the slicer and, sure enough, the next loaf was already through the knives with another one coming behind it. I flung the first loaf onto the plastic bread rack and then reached for the next one.

"Hey, easy on the merchandise!" Marcel said.

"Sorry," I muttered. This time when I went to slide the loaf into the bag, I must have clipped something because instead of the loaf going into the bag, the bag went shooting off across the bakery, landing on a table where one of the bakers was rolling out pie dough. She scowled at me and then swiped it off the table, hardly breaking her rhythm as she did.

"Don't rush it," Marcel said as another bag automatically inflated. "Just take your time and do it right."

Take my time? Do it right? I wanted to tell him I could do one or the other, but the loaves were already stacking up on me, and there was no time to say anything.

"Hurry!" Marcel said. "They're going to fall onto the floor!"

I grabbed the next loaf, but in my rush I must have squeezed it too hard because as I swung it toward the bagger, it exploded like a stack of playing cards in a game of fifty-two pickup, bread slices flying everywhere.

"Uh-oh," I mumbled.

"Hey, what the heck are you doing over there?" Lucas asked, sticking his head out from behind the machine.

"Don't worry about the mess," Marcel said. "Just get the next one."

It was hard not to worry about the loaf I had just wasted. I hoped Marcel wasn't going to take it out of my pay. Then again, the last thing I cared about at that point was money. I just wanted the torture to stop.

I managed to pick up the next loaf without it exploding, and this time I even got it into the bag, but by the time I put the bread clip on, two more loaves had come through, and before I could grab the next one, it fell onto the floor. I couldn't believe it. I'd hardly been working for more than a few minutes, and I was already costing Marcel more than he was paying me.

"Step aside for a moment," Marcel said, taking my place. "Lucas, you can stop loading!"

Marcel bagged the remaining loaves and put

them on the rack in no time flat. Then he shut off the bread slicer and turned to me. "You know what, Wyatt? I think I have a better job for you."

"A better job?" I asked. "What about Lucas?"

"He can stay here," Marcel said. "Come with me."

I gave Lucas a helpless look as Marcel led me back toward the ovens. All Lucas could do was shrug. Was I already being demoted? Was Marcel going to call my mom to pick me up? Why couldn't Lucas have been the bagger instead of me? As much as I didn't want the job, now that I was there, I didn't want to be fired either.

That is, until I found out what Marcel had in store for me next.

- 10 -

"So, all I have to do is grease these things?" I asked, eyeing a stack of stove-blackened bread pans, each of which could bake four loaves at a time. That didn't sound too bad.

"That's right," Marcel said. "For starters. Once you finish this stack, you can get started on those." He pointed to several monumental stacks right between two boiling-hot ovens. My shoulders slumped. This was going to take me forever. And I already had sweat streaming down my back.

"Just dip this rag into this bucket, then swipe it around the inside of the pan—all four sides and the bottom. And you gotta make sure you don't miss any spots because if there's one thing I hate, it's bread sticking in the pan. Got it?"

"Got it," I replied, even though I didn't quite get it yet. "Can you show me again?"

"Bottom, side, side, side, side," he said, whipping the grease-soaked rag around like he had been born doing it. In a flash, he had all four compartments greased up and ready to go. Then he wrapped his hand in his apron and picked up the pan, depositing it on a trolley, which I assumed someone could wheel away when it was full.

"You'll have to wear an oven mitt on one hand," he said, holding one out to me. It used to be white, but now it was pretty much black due to countless scorch marks. "These pans are hot, straight out of the oven, and I don't want you to burn yourself."

From slicing bread to greasing hot pans next to two blazing hot ovens—I had definitely been demoted.

"Okay, think you can handle it?" Marcel asked.

"Definitely," I said, trying to sound as confident as possible as I took the oven mitt and the rag from him.

THE BIG TWITCH

"I'll hang around for a moment just to be sure," he said.

I had been hoping to avoid that.

Thankfully, greasing pans was as easy as it looked. What wasn't easy was doing it without getting scorched. Even with the oven mitt, I would accidentally bump one of the hot pans with my forearm and yelp in pain, only to jerk my arm and hit another pan, burning my arm yet again.

"I'll go get you a baker's jacket to protect your arms," Marcel said after the third time I managed to singe myself. "Other than that, you're doing great!"

It was nice to get a compliment, but I figured he was just being nice. By that point I didn't care, though. All I wanted was to finish the job and get out of there. And in my head, I vowed I was never coming back.

True to his word, at the end of our four-hour shift, Marcel offered us all the donuts we could eat—mostly seconds, deformed donuts that they couldn't sell. But as tired and hungry as I was, I couldn't even look at a donut, never mind eat one. As for Lucas, he scarfed down half a dozen and then took one for the road. That guy was a bottomless pit!

"So, how was your first shift?" Mom asked as Lucas and I piled into the van. "Whew!" she exclaimed before we had a chance to respond. "You guys stink! I don't even know if I want those clothes in my van, never mind the house. When we get home, it's straight to the shower for both of you!"

"Yes, ma'am," Lucas replied through a mouthful of apple fritter, sounding as cheerful as ever. "And to answer your question," he added once he swallowed, "it was great!"

Mom glanced at me in the rearview mirror as she pulled away from the bakery. "How about you, Wyatt?"

I shook my head. "All I want is a shower—and my bed!"

It was bad enough that the job had eaten up my entire morning, but it wound up consuming half of my afternoon too. After taking a shower and eating a snack, I popped in my AirPods, put on an episode of one of my favorite video game podcasts, and then laid on my bed, planning to close my eyes for just a few minutes—only to wake up three hours later!

I couldn't believe it. I leaped out of bed and raced out of my room, hoping to spend what remained of the afternoon gaming. But on my way through the kitchen, my dad intercepted me.

"Wyatt! Just the person I wanted to see."

I barely slowed down, swiping an orange out of the fruit bowl on the island before heading toward the basement.

"Good to see you too, Dad. Gotta go."

"Hold on a second, Wyatt."

I stopped short on the top step of the basement stairs. "Yeah?"

"Forgetting something?"

I scrunched my eyebrows together, trying to figure out what he was talking about.

"The orange. You weren't planning to eat that in your precious gaming room, were you?"

I looked down at it. "Oh, uh, no, I guess not." I sped over to the sink and peeled the orange as fast as I could before he had a chance to tell me why he was so glad to see me.

"I didn't think so. Anyway, when you're done with that, before you disappear downstairs, I have a few chores I need you to help me with."

I threw my head back in frustration, nearly dropping the orange into the sink. "Seriously? I already worked all morning, and then I accidentally fell asleep. I was just going to do some gaming with my—"

"Gaming can wait. There's rain in the forecast, and I have some yard work I want to finish before it starts to pour. Now, come on. It won't take long."

All I could do was clench my teeth in frustration. Would I ever be able to get back to gaming?

Two hours later—after helping my dad clean the gutters, prune our fruit trees, and mow the lawn—it started to rain, so he finally let me free. By then it was nearly 5:00.

I dashed back inside. This time when I passed through the kitchen, Mom was there, cooking up a storm. Spaghetti and meat sauce—one of my least favorite meals. Couldn't anything go my way for once?

THE BIG TWITCH

"Supper'll be ready in fifteen minutes, Wyatt, so don't get caught up in a game," Mom said as I headed toward the stairs.

"I won't," I said, taking my frustration out on each step.

"Shh . . ." Olivia hissed, meeting me halfway up. "Where do you think you're going?"

"Excuse me?" I said, unable to believe the little pipsqueak was blocking my way. "Where does it look like I'm going?"

"Well, for starters, you sound like a pack of angry rhinos."

I wasn't surprised. I *felt* like a pack of angry rhinos.

"But besides that, Lucas is sleeping."

"So what?" I said. "It's nearly time for supper. He's going to have to wake up soon anyway."

I went to move past her, but she held out her arm to stop me. "Seriously, Wyatt, have some consideration for others."

All I could do was stare at her in disbelief. Was the entire world out to stop me from gaming?

"Move your arm. Now," I said, hoping she

heard the warning in my voice. She did, but she also shook her head at me in disgust.

"Some people's children."

"We have the same parents!" I shouted back at her as I bounded down to the bottom of the steps.

"Prove it!" she called after me.

I didn't dignify that comment with a response.

When I got to my gaming room, I was surprised to find Lucas not in his bed but in front of his computer.

"I thought you were sleeping," I said.

He glanced up at me. "Oh, I just told Olivia I was tired to get her off my back. No offense, but . . ." He glanced at the stairs and lowered his voice. "She can be a little much sometimes, you know?"

"Tell me about it," I replied as I plopped into my chair and put on my headphones.

"Want to jump into a game?" Lucas asked.

"Can't," I replied. "Mom's going to call us for supper in a few minutes."

Instead of logging into *Rumble Royale*, I went to the streamer's YouTube channel to see if he had posted any videos of him and his team playing on

THE BIG TWITCH

the new map. I figured it was a good way to learn the map while also getting his take on it. Sure enough, there were plenty of videos, including a couple of them taking on the Ghost Gate and Helheim. I was about to press "play," hoping I could watch one of them before supper, when a voice way too close to my head nearly caused me to fall out of my chair.

"I still don't know what you see in that guy," Lucas said. Once I recovered, I looked up at where he was standing, peering over my shoulder.

"And I still don't see what you have against him," I replied. "Do you believe everything you read online?"

"Not everything. Just what I hear about him."

"You still haven't shown me where you heard he's such a terrible person."

He shrugged as he headed for the stairs. "I have my sources."

When he was gone, I turned back to my screen, but just as I was about to press "play" on a video, I hesitated. Then I opened a search window and entered the streamer's name, determined to get to the bottom of what Lucas was talking about.

- 11 -

Even though I'd had the rest of Saturday and Sunday to get up to speed on the new *Rumble Royale* map, by the time Monday rolled around, I still didn't feel like I was anywhere close to ready for my tryout. It didn't help that I was exhausted from having to wake up early—again. Plus, the bit of research I'd done on the streamer had raised a few red flags. I had found the comment thread that Lucas was talking about, and even though I didn't want to believe what the poster said, even I had to admit his accusations didn't sound like something a person would just make up.

THE BIG TWITCH

Still, it was only one side of the story, so I decided to give the streamer the benefit of the doubt. But it was hard, and it was throwing off my game.

"Come on, Wyatt," Lucas said when I died early in a box fight against a total bot during our practice before school that morning. "You should have nailed that guy."

"I know," I replied.

"If I didn't know better, I'd say you're *trying* to lose," he added.

Before I could respond, my headphones pinged with a text message from Darian. He was still doing his "vow of silence" thing.

Everything OK?

Yeah, I replied. *Just tired.*

Well, if you want to talk, I'm always available to listen.

Even though he couldn't see my face, I was certain that Darian could tell that something was up. He had a sort of sixth sense about that kind of thing. Maybe all that mindfulness really did work in some weird sort of way.

Thanks.

KEVIN MILLER

School that day was a total snooze fest—almost literally for me, as I caught myself dozing off several times.

As the time for my audition approached that afternoon, however, I was so jittery it felt like I had just downed three Red Bulls, one after another. Thankfully, Lucas had a marathon session with his tabletop gaming club lined up, so I wouldn't have to worry about him interfering. That meant Olivia would probably stay out of my hair too. She only tended to come downstairs when Lucas was there. Plus, it was raining outside, so Dad couldn't put me to work. And Mom was out grocery shopping. It couldn't have been a better setup.

One minute before showtime, I put on my headphones and logged on. No sooner had I entered the lobby than the streamer and the rest of his squad showed up.

"Yo, KwyattWyatt, great to meet you," he said.

"Great to meet you too," I replied, unable to believe I was actually talking to him. I'd watched so many of his streams and videos that it felt like I knew him already, but it was still strange to think

THE BIG TWITCH

he was talking to *me*.

"I know you're probably feeling a bit of pressure right now, but I just want you to relax and have fun, okay?"

"Okay," I replied.

See? I told myself. *This guy isn't so bad.*

"Before we get started, let me introduce you to the rest of the crew. Geared4War, meet KwyattWyatt."

Geared4War's avatar did a little dance for me in greeting. His skin looked like a fish wearing a beanie, and he had a golf club for a sledgehammer.

"And this here is BrittleGremlin," the streamer said. His avatar was a wiener that was wearing a hot dog bun for a vest, a backward cap, sunglasses, chains around his neck, and a swirl of yellow mustard down his chest. He did a dance for me as well.

"And you know who I am," the streamer said, shooting my avatar several times just for fun. The skin he was wearing was a girl in a skintight gray ninja suit. "So, let's get this party started!"

As soon as we were on the War Wagon, heading toward the island, I tried to relax, telling myself this was just another game. The problem was, it *wasn't* just another game, and every part of my body—especially my sweating palms—was all too aware of that.

"Okay, KW, why don't you choose where we should drop?" the streamer said. I was so nervous it took me a second to realize he was talking to me—KW being a shortened version of my gamertag.

Great, I thought. *This is my first test.* As I'd taught my team, knowing where to drop was one of the most important decisions a player could make in the game. I already had my favorite spots, but the question was, which point of interest (POI) was *his* favorite?

"Time's ticking, KW," Geared4War said in a sing-song voice.

"Sorry, uh, why don't we head for Asgard?" I said and then cringed, wishing I had said "Helheim."

"Good choice," the streamer replied, which caused my tense shoulders to relax somewhat. "People are all Ghost Gate this, Helheim that, but Asgard is the bomb. Let's go!"

As we jumped out of the War Wagon and our gliders deployed, I felt like I really was walking on

THE BIG TWITCH

air. I had passed my first test!

"So, which building on Asgard do you like best?" the streamer asked, probably trying to assess my decision-making once again.

My brain scrambled to come up with an answer. Apart from the huge statue of Odin overlooking everything, Asgard was broken up into four separate areas—the north hall, the main square, Odin's throne room, and the south hall.

"Actually," I said, still having not quite made up my mind but feeling a need to fill the dead air, "I kind of like Odin's throne room."

"Boom! What did I tell you, boys? KW is the man! Let's do it!"

Despite my nervousness, I felt a smile break out on my face. I was two for two!

"Just out of curiosity, why did you choose that spot?" the streamer asked.

Oh, boy. Another test. I'd hardly had a moment to recover from the first two.

"Uh, well, it's a bit isolated from the other buildings, which means fewer players tend to go there. Plus, there are four chests in the building, including one god chest in a hidden room that you can access right away, so it's easy to loot."

"I like it, I like it. What else?"

"If you work your way down through the floors, you can get all four chests before the game even starts. And on the main floor, you can build between the pillars, so you can safely pop some heals down there before you head out. Most buildings don't allow you to do that."

"Nice. Lead the way!"

We ditched our gliders and landed on a small balcony on the outside of Odin's throne room. I ran straight to where I knew a chest was hidden behind a couple of clay pots and opened it. An AR, some ammo, and a few mats popped out. I was about to grab it, but then I stopped.

"Yo, you want that gun?" I said, offering it up to the streamer.

"No, you take it," he said. "See if you can beam some kids out of the air while we loot the rest of this joint, then join us on the main floor."

"Got it," I replied, scanning the sky. I took a few potshots at some players who were gliding down, scoring a few hits but no kills. But when a few bullets flew my way, I booked it down through the hole that the others had hacked through the floor, then took the zip line down to the main floor. They had already boxed up and were popping meds.

"Here, KW," the streamer said, tossing me a chug splash. "Drink up!"

I did just that, popping a med kit I had picked up from the first chest as well.

"So, now what?" I said once we were all juiced up.

I could almost hear the excitement crackling in the streamer's voice. "Time to go hunting!"

He and the others smashed through the walls they had built and began combing through the other buildings on Asgard, looking for other squads to pick off.

Right away, we stumbled across two teams who were engaged in a wicked firefight. We opened fire on one of them, and I scored the winning shot, taking out the last man standing.

"Way to go, KW!" the streamer said. "Nice shooting."

The rest of the game went just as well, with our

team making kill after kill after kill. I'd never played so aggressively before. It was like a dream come true. The fear and anxiety I had felt earlier was nowhere to be found. Instead, I felt more confident than ever before—invincible, even. With these guys at my side, there was no one we couldn't beat. Rather than avoiding fights, these guys sought them out. And no wonder. It seemed like they—correction, *we*—couldn't lose.

By the time we got to end game, all four of us were still alive, which was a first for me. At that point the circle had shrunk to a small spot just outside of Lavish Lair, a huge Gothic castle with towers and a solarium and dozens of chimneys sticking up from the roof. We leaped and climbed, built and smashed and fired away as we tried to take out the other remaining players. In the midst of the chaos, Geared4War and BrittleGremlin both got killed.

"Just you and me now, kid!" the streamer yelled as the circle moved yet again.

Almost out of mats and ammo but desperate to stay alive, I sledgehammered a kid who was weak and took him out. And just in time too. Someone

THE BIG TWITCH

else jumped into his box, but I grabbed the dead kid's gun and took the other player out just in time.

Before I realized what was happening, a blue banner with "#1 Victory Royale" was floating on the screen in front of me. My mouth fell open in disbelief.

"Way to go, KW! Last man standing," the streamer said. In all the chaos, I hadn't even noticed he had been taken out too.

"Really? Wow. Great work, team," I said, wanting to make sure I didn't hog all the credit. "So, uh, what do we do now? Jump into another game?"

"Naw, I gotta bail," the streamer said.

"Okay, no problem," I said. "But before you go, can you tell me if . . . well . . . did I make the team?"

He laughed in what I told myself wasn't a mocking tone. "We'll be in touch, amigo. Seacrest . . . out!"

I won't deny it; I felt a bit deflated afterward. I was pretty sure he was happy with how I had played—I'd gotten six kills in total, including the winning one—but I had thought that maybe they'd want to hang out and chat a bit afterwards or something. Get to know each other. I tried to brush it off, though, telling myself he probably had to talk things over with his teammates before making a decision.

I logged out of the game, then took off my headphones and stared at my monitor. Had that really just happened?

"Enjoy your game?" an all-too-familiar voice said, nearly scaring me to death once again. How did such a big, lanky guy always manage to sneak up on me like that?

I spun my chair toward Lucas, hoping he didn't notice the blush creeping into my cheeks. I felt like I'd just been caught cheating on a test—not that I'd ever done that. "Um, I thought you had an epic Warhammer sesh scheduled for today."

"So did I," Lucas replied. "Guess I got the date wrong."

We were both silent as he took a bite out of an apple I hadn't realized he was holding, then he just continued to stand there, staring at me.

"So . . . how much of the game did you see?" I asked.

"Enough," he said, taking another bite. Then he sauntered over to his side of the room, grabbed his backpack, and started stuffing some things into

THE BIG TWITCH

it, including clothes, books, and his sleeping bag, which he attached on the outside.

"Hey, what are you doing?" I asked.

He didn't answer until backpack was full. Then he slung it over his shoulder and headed for the stairs. "Tell Olivia she won't have to bother cleaning up down here for a few days," Lucas said. "In fact, she may never have to do it again."

"Wait a second. Where are you going?" I asked, leaping out of my chair and following him to the stairs. Lucas stopped at the top and looked back down at me.

"I don't know," he replied. "I just thought you'd like a bit of alone time with your team... your new team, that is."

Before I had a chance to reply, he was gone.

As I stood there at the bottom of the stairs, the elation I'd felt just a few short minutes ago was gone, replaced by a pit in the bottom of my stomach that felt like it was going to swallow me.

What had I done?

- 12 -

The next day, I decided to ditch our early morning practice, unable to face the rest of the team. I didn't even bother to text them, certain that Lucas had already told them what was going on. I would have ditched school too if my parents had let me, but I knew *that* wasn't going to happen.

I managed to avoid the other members of the Stream Team all morning, seeing as we didn't have any classes together. When noon arrived, I was planning to eat my lunch outside rather than in the cafeteria, even if it meant eating on my own. However, just as I was about to make my getaway . . .

THE BIG TWITCH

"Yo, Wyatt!"

I froze, my hand on the door that would have taken me outside. Why hadn't I left two seconds sooner?

I turned around. It was Darian. Of course he'd *today* to break his vow of silence.

"Where you going?" he asked as he approached me.

"Me? Oh, uh, nowhere," I said, removing my hand from the door handle.

"How come you didn't show up for practice this morning?" he asked as he started toward the cafeteria, assuming I would follow him. I did, hurrying to catch up. "Between the three of us, we probably texted you, like, fifty times."

I'd been so scared to see their reaction to me trying out for the other team that I hadn't dared to check my phone. "Oh, uh, you know, I slept in."

Darian nodded. "That's what I figured. Probably tired from the new job, huh?"

"Uh, yeah," I said, still trying to figure out if Lucas had told him about my tryout. "It was pretty tragic."

"I'll bet," Darian replied, grinning.

When we got to our usual table, Shu and Lucas

were already there. Shu smiled and waved, just like she always did.

"Hello, guys!" Her English was getting better all the time, though her accent was still pretty strong.

"Hi, Shu," I said. "How'd the table tennis tournament go over the weekend?" With everything else happening in my life, I'd nearly forgotten about it. I felt guilty for not going to the tournament to cheer her on. "Did watching all that film help?"

She grinned and then reached into her pocket and pulled out a bright red ribbon, at the end of which was hanging a shiny gold medal.

THE BIG TWITCH

"Way to go!" I said, giving her a fist bump.

"Showoff," Lucas said between bites, shoveling his lunch down, as usual. Still grinning, Shu nudged him with her shoulder, and he nudged her back.

"Sleep in this morning?" Shu asked.

"Something like that," I muttered, casting a glance at Lucas, but he wasn't paying any attention to me. Instead, he high-fived one of his tabletop gaming buddies as he passed by. "So, uh, how'd you guys do this morning?"

"We got slaughtered," Lucas said, casting an accusing glare at me.

"Sorry about that," I said. "I didn't mean to let you all down. It won't happen again."

"Guess it's true what they say, huh?" Darian said. "There's no 'I' in 'team.'"

Just then the bell rang to signal the start of intramurals. Lucas gathered his things and wiped his mouth as he stood up; he was scheduled to play dodgeball. "No, but there is an 'I' in 'win.' Isn't that right, Wyatt?"

Before I could answer, he was gone.

"What was that all about?" Darian asked.

Realizing he and Shu were both giving me a strange look, all I could do was shrug as I unwrapped my sandwich. "Who knows? This is Lucas we're talking about, right?"

The others chuckled, then just like that, it was like everything was back to normal again. For the first time in the past sixteen hours or so, I felt like I could relax. I just hoped the feeling would last.

When I got home from school that day, I raced to my gaming room, eager to hop onto Discord to see if the streamer had sent me a message. I would have checked it on my phone, but my parents had forced me to remove Discord and every other social media app after attending a parents' information night warning about the dangers of social media. That only added to my mom's dislike of technology and her feeling that it was taking over people's lives—particularly mine.

When I got downstairs, I pulled up short. Not only was the light on, Lucas was lying on his bed and eating a snack, as usual.

"Back so soon?" I said, trying to suppress the

excitement that had been coursing through my veins just a few seconds ago. "I thought you were gone for good."

He shrugged as he crammed a handful of crackers into his mouth. "I didn't want Olivia or your parents to worry."

I nodded. That made sense. But something else didn't.

"You didn't tell Shu and Darian."

"Nope."

"Why not?"

"Because that's *your* job, not mine."

Oh.

"Right. Uh, thanks, I guess."

I slumped into my gaming chair as I processed that. I was dying to boot up my computer, but I didn't want Lucas to know how excited I was. Everything I'd ever dreamed of—fame, fortune, a chance to travel the world playing in the biggest gaming tournaments—the key to all of that and more could be waiting in my inbox. All I had to do was turn on my computer.

"It's okay. You can see if your little buddy sent

you a message," Lucas said. "I won't peek."

It was that obvious, huh?

Bending down, I hit the "power" button, then waited as my computer sprang to life. I logged into Discord, and sure enough, I had several messages waiting for me. I scanned through them, then my breath caught in my throat. One of them was from the streamer.

Despite my excitement, I hesitated to click on it, not daring to believe he would actually invite me to join his team but not knowing what I would do if he didn't.

"Would you just click on it already?" Lucas asked, having gotten off his bed and approached my desk without me noticing—again!

I arched an eyebrow at him. "I thought you said you weren't going to peek."

He shrugged. "I lied."

Turning back to my computer, my hand hovered over my mouse for a second, then I clicked on the link.

I don't remember much of what it said beyond the first word, but I'll never forget what that word was.

THE BIG TWITCH

Congratulations!

"So, Wyatt, looks like you have a decision to make," Lucas said, retreating to his bed. "I can't wait to see how Shu and Darian react—and let's not forget Olivia."

Olivia. Oh, yeah. She wasn't going to like this. She wasn't going to like it one little bit.

- 13 -

I had considered breaking the news to Shu and Darian (and Olivia, seeing as she always seemed to be listening in) the following morning at practice, but then I decided against it, thinking it might go over better if I told them in person. That morning's session went surprisingly well, especially now that Darian was talking again. We actually made it to the top ten. And for a moment, I felt wistful about what might have been. All three of them had come so far since we started.

Later that morning as I approached school, my stomach was in knots, worried about how Dar-

THE BIG TWITCH

ian and Shu would react. I hoped they wouldn't hate me. Now that I'd gone from having next to no friends to having a handful of people who were starting to feel like the real thing, I was in no hurry to return to my solitary ways.

Though I had intended to keep a low profile for the morning, thinking the best time to tell them was during lunch, the moment I entered the halls I could tell something was up. As I passed, groups of people looked at me and smiled. And a kid who used to bully me in elementary school reached out to give me a fist bump.

"Congrats, Wyatt!" he said.

I returned the gesture, mystified and a bit worried it was part of some sort of elaborate prank. What had I done to deserve such attention?

The answer came when I arrived at my locker and found Darian, Shu, and Lucas waiting for me, and they didn't look happy.

"Care to explain this?" Darian asked, holding up his phone so I could see the screen. At that moment I wished *I* had taken a vow of silence.

I squinted at his phone, and only then did I

realize what all the fuss was about. The streamer had announced my addition to the team that morning, and it was all over social media. Why hadn't he warned me he was going to do that? Then I realized he probably had. I just hadn't checked my Discord messages yet.

"Yo, Wyatt, way to go!" an older kid said, reaching out for a high-five.

"Thanks," I said, smacking his hand as he walked past, though my heart wasn't in it.

"Just for the record, I wasn't the one who told

them," Lucas said, pointing his index fingers at Darian and Shu's heads and then backing away so I had to face them on my own.

"Obviously," I muttered.

"So, is it true?" Darian asked.

I looked between him and Shu. She was scowling at me with her arms crossed, a table tennis paddle in each hand. I hoped she wasn't planning to use them on me.

"Well, not officially," I said. "I mean, he made me an offer, yeah, but I haven't signed a contract or anything."

"But he's already announced it," Darian said, "which must mean you plan to join his team."

I thought about it for a second and then shrugged. I didn't know what to say.

"So, that's it? You're ditching us?"

"Yeah, you ditching us?" Shu asked, narrowing her eyes.

"No, of course not," I said.

"But if you're playing with them, how can you play with *us*?" Darian said. "Not only will you not have time, I'm sure there'll be a clause in the contract forbidding it."

All I could do was shrug again. I didn't know the answer, but I was pretty certain he was right.

"I can't believe it," Darian said, shaking his head. "And here I thought we were friends."

"But we *are* friends," I said, desperate to convince them of that. "Speaking of which, don't friends support each other when a good opportunity comes along? I mean, yeah, I understand why you guys are disappointed, but on the other hand, I thought you'd be, I don't know, I thought you'd be happy for me."

"Friends stick together, Wyatt. They don't ditch each other the moment something better comes along."

"Nobody's ditching anyone," I said. "We can still hang out together, and we can still game together. Just not, you know, professionally."

"But that was the whole point of forming the Stream Team," Darian replied. "This was your dream, Wyatt, but you made it ours."

I looked down at my shoes and nodded. "I know."

"I suppose this means you're going to ditch the

THE BIG TWITCH

Medi-Taters too, huh?" Darian said.

I looked up at him. "No, of course not." To be fair, though, that would have been a nice bonus.

Darian sniffed. "I'll believe that when I see it. Well, I guess that's it then," he said, turning to walk away. "Catch you later, Wyatt."

"Wait, don't go. We can—" My voice was cut off by the bell signaling it was time to get to our home rooms. Shu gave me a disappointed look and then followed Darian down the hall.

As I watched them go, a hand clamped down on my shoulder.

"That certainly could have gone better," Lucas replied, smiling. I glowered at him. Why did he have to be so glib about everything? "Catch you on the flippity-flip," he said, releasing my shoulder and moseying down the hall, bumping shoulders with a group of his tabletop gaming buddies.

I stood there in the rapidly vacating hallway, watching as my former teammates melted into the crowd. Despite the amazing opportunity that had come my way, I couldn't help but feel like I was right back where I was before this whole Stream

KEVIN MILLER

Team thing started.

Alone.

"What's the matter, Kelsey?" a gruff voice asked. "Someone glue your shoes to the floor?" I turned to see Mr. Daviduke approaching, a whistle around his neck and his lips pursed in dissatisfaction beneath his bristling mustache.

"No, sir," I replied.

"Then get to your homeroom—unless you've always harbored a secret wish to sweep and polish my gym floor!"

"No, sir," I replied, hustling off.

"Oh, and Kelsey," he said, causing me to slow down and glance back.

"Yes?"

"Congratulations on making the team."

"Thank you, sir," I replied, surprised that he knew about it too.

"Not that I consider esports to be *real* sports—not even close—but if you're ever in need of a coach, you know where to find me. I may not look like it, but I was quite the Xbox junkie back in the day."

"I didn't realize that, sir," I replied. "Thank you!"

As I hurried off to class, I couldn't help but smile. At least *someone* was still in my corner—even if he did scare me to death.

- 14 -

That night at supper, I finally shared the news with my parents. At first they were confused, especially my mom.

"Contract? What sort of contract? What are you talking about?" she asked.

"This guy runs a professional esports team," I explained for what felt like the tenth time, "and he wants me to join it."

"But what does that *mean?*" she asked, still not getting it. "Does he want you to move somewhere or . . ."

"No. At least, not yet. Of course, every once in a

THE BIG TWITCH

while I might have to travel for an in-person tournament or something, but for the time being, I can play right here from home."

"And he's going to *pay* you to do this?"

"Yes—I mean no. That is, if we win a tournament, we'll share the prize money, but it's not like I'll be on a monthly salary or anything."

"But isn't that what you were trying to do with your friends? Make it big as a professional gamer?"

"Yeah, kind of, but with this guy I have a much better chance."

"Why?"

"Because his teammates are—" I stopped short and looked at Lucas, having almost forgotten he was there. He and Olivia were both scowling at me as they awaited my answer. "They're professionals," I said, hoping it wasn't too obvious what I had *meant* to say—"Because his teammates are *good*."

My mom shook her head. "I don't know, Wyatt. What do you think, Richard?"

My dad shrugged as he used his knife to push some rice onto his fork. I could tell he didn't want to get into it with her. "I mean, it sounds legit, but before Wyatt signs anything, we'll have to get a lawyer to look things over."

"Lawyers cost money," Mom reminded him.

"But, Mom, I could make a lot of money doing this. Huge money."

"I still don't like it," she said. "It seems way too easy. It sounds like a scam or something. I'm worried this guy is just trying to take advantage of you."

"Easy?" I said, latching onto that one word. "Do you have any idea how long I've been training for this? How hard I've worked?"

Mom scoffed. "I'd hardly call sitting in front of a computer for hours playing some silly game 'work.'"

"The game isn't silly, Mom. Millions of people play it, and the company that makes it is worth thirty-two billion dollars and employs thousands of people. And besides, isn't that what Dad does all day? Sit in front of a computer for hours? You don't call that work? He seems to get paid pretty well for it." My dad was an accountant for a large construction firm.

"Oh, Wyatt, that's hardly the same—"

"You know what?" I said, setting my cutlery

down. "I'm sick of you always dissing the things I love. I don't do that to you or Dad or Olivia. This has been my dream for as long as I can remember, and it's finally coming true. Why can't you just be happy for me? Why can't *any* of you be happy for me?" I glared at Olivia and Lucas in particular to emphasize my point. Both of them lowered their eyes to their plates.

"You know what else?" I said, working up a real head of steam. "I don't care what you say. I'm signing that contract whether you like it or not, and I'm going pro. And when I do make it big, you're all going to wish you'd been nicer to me. A lot nicer!"

With that, I got up and stormed out of the dining room. I'd never done anything like that before, and I'd *never* spoken to either of my parents that way. To be honest, I felt a little sick inside at the look on my parents' faces, knowing I couldn't take back my words or the harsh way I'd said them.

But I was angry too. And I really was sick and tired of having to defend the things I loved. If my friends and family weren't going to support me, so be it. I had a new team who would, and I couldn't wait to join them and prove the rest of the world wrong.

Keep an eye out for book 4 in the Game On series, coming soon!

About the Author

Kevin Miller is an award-winning novelist and filmmaker. Over the past 30 years, he has applied his craft to a wide range of projects, including feature films, documentaries, novels, non-fiction books, and comic books. He has also taught creative writing across Canada, the US, and in the UK and Australia. Kevin has been featured on CNN, CBC Radio, and numerous other radio and TV outlets and podcasts, and his work has been written about and reviewed in dozens of publications, including the *New York Times*, *Variety*, and the *Globe and Mail*. Kevin lives in Kimberley, BC, with his wife and four kids. When he's not writing, he enjoys playing hockey, skateboarding, fishing, hiking, and otherwise exploring his world. To learn more about Kevin, visit www.bakkenbooks.com and www.kevinmillerxi.com.